NIGHT CITY

WORDS BY **MONICA WELLINGTON** WITH **ANDREW KUPFER**

PICTURES BY **MONICA WELLINGTON**

DUTTON CHILDREN'S BOOKS ■ NEW YORK

OFFEE

TAXI

■ FOR LYDIA ■

Text copyright © 1998 by Monica Wellington and Andrew Kupfer
Illustrations copyright © 1998 by Monica Wellington

CIP Data is available.
Published in the United States 1998 by Dutton Children's Books,
a member of Penguin Putnam Inc.
375 Hudson Street, New York, New York 10014

Designed by Amy Berniker
Printed in Hong Kong
First Edition
ISBN 0-525-45948-0
10 9 8 7 6 5 4 3 2 1

Gouache was used to create the full-color art for this book.

The sun falls. Darkness rises. You sleep, and dream, snug beneath your covers. But the city outside your window doesn't rest at night. Its soaring towers glow. Its people work—no matter what the hour.

Night ty

At seven o'clock, the dancers practice in their rehearsal studio for tonight's performance. One last time, the ballet master helps them learn their steps. Soon they'll take their places on the stage before the eyes of the eager audience. The orchestra will start to play. The dancers will forget their nervousness and twirl with artistry and grace.

At eight o'clock, the travelers arrive at their hotel, weary from their long and tiring journey. The staff welcomes them and makes them feel at home. The desk attendant checks them in. The porter helps them with their bags. The elevator operator whooshes them to their rooms and to the soft, plump pillows of their beds.

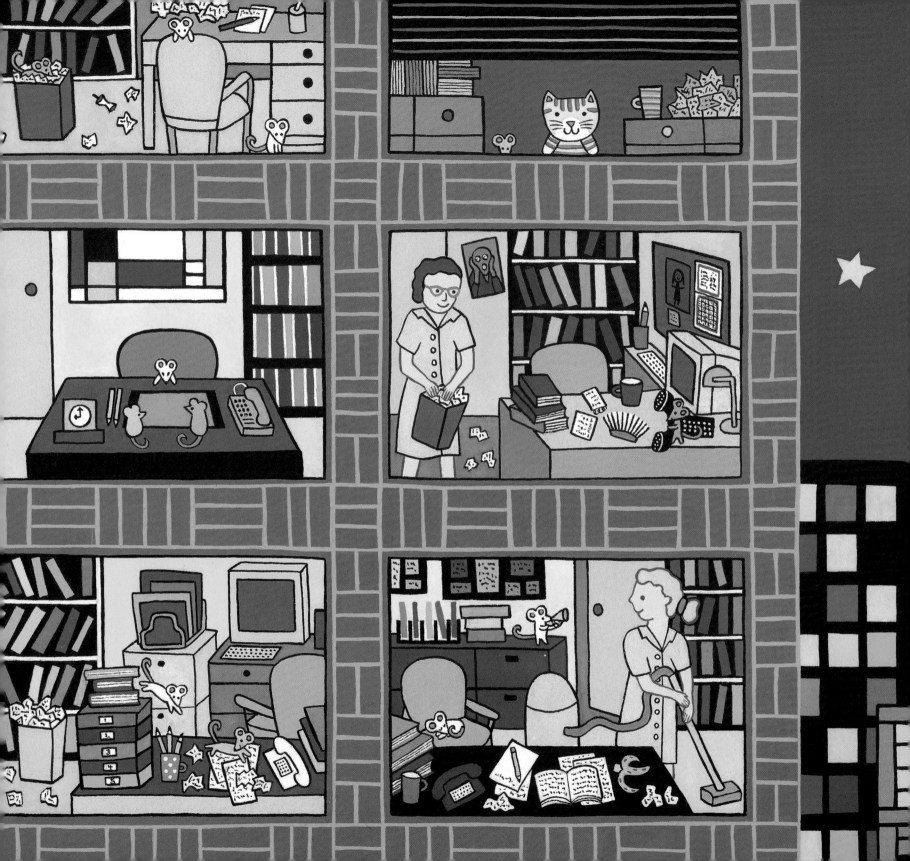

At nine o'clock, cleaners clear the messes left each day in the city's office buildings. They empty bins of trash. They pick up scattered papers and morsels of snacks that have fallen on the floor. They vacuum, sweep, wipe, and polish. And when they leave, the offices are clean and shiny, ready for the next day.

At ten o'clock, the artist is working in her studio. She lives there, too, so she can paint at any hour. She squeezes tubes of oil paint to make a rainbow on her palette, then creates a swirl of colors on her canvas. Her inspiration is the sparkling city skyline, the buildings lit like jewels against the dark of night. She paints what she sees with her eyes—and with her imagination.

At eleven o'clock, sirens shriek and wail as a fire engine races to a blaze. The firefighters aim their water hoses at the flames. They scramble up ladders braced against the burning building and break through windows, rushing inside to rescue anyone who may be trapped. They save lives and douse the flames.

At twelve o'clock, the watchman makes his rounds in the art museum. All night long he guards the treasures there, his solitary footsteps the only sound that breaks the hush. He searches with his flashlight for intruders who might try to steal the valuable artwork. He hopes the only other eyes he sees tonight are in the paintings on the wall.

At one o'clock, in the quiet of the night, people bring their cargo to the city in many different ways. Boats sail on the darkened river. An airplane flies across the starry sky. A freight train steams along the railroad tracks. And a truck trundles over the lonely bridge to the city's produce market.

At two o'clock, the newspaper is rolling off the printing press. Reporters have worked frantically to write their articles before the deadline. Now the pressmen operate the thundering machinery that turns the giant rolls of newsprint into news-papers. By morning, trucks will bring them to every newsstand in the city.

At three o'clock, musicians in the nightclub play their instruments and fill the air with liquid sound. The rhythms of the music pull the dancers from their seats. They laugh and shout—singing, clapping, spinning ever faster as the night goes on.

At four o'clock, the police officer patrols the avenues. Up and down he slowly drives, closely watching any shadow that might cloak a robber or a thief. Who knows where trouble may be lurking? Does anyone need help? The officer will try to keep the streets safe all night long.

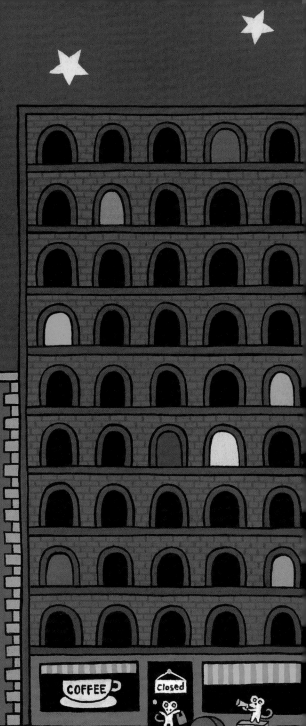

At five o'clock, the bakers make fresh buns and bread and pastries. They mix flour, yeast, and other ingredients. Then they knead and shape the pliant dough. In the oven, the rounded loaves begin to rise and fill the air with their delicious fragrance. Then out they come, all crusty, warm, and golden brown, ready for your morning jam and butter.

SUGAR

YUM

At six o'clock, the vendors in the market are setting up their stalls. The market swells with fruits and vegetables to buy. Strawberries and eggplants and potatoes come from farms near-by, the soil of country fields still fresh upon them. Pineapples, bananas, and papayas come from countries far away. Soon the market will be ready for the bustling crowds.

At seven o'clock, the sun is rising. The night workers are tired and hungry. They come to the diner to fill their rumbling stomachs when their shifts are over. The waitress takes their orders. She, too, has worked all night. Her aching feet cry out for rest. Nobody has much to say. The night workers are ready to go home and sleep.

Morning comes. Darkness falls away. You wake and rub your eyes and stretch and yawn. But the city never went to sleep. People worked at every hour…and will again tonight.